CAN YOU
SNORE
LIKE A DINOSAUR?

The Castle Point Books trademark is owned by Castle Point Publications, LLC.
Castle Point books are published and distributed by St. Martin's Press.

www.castlepointbooks.com
www.stmartins.com

The Library of Congress Cataloging-in-Publication Data is available upon request

ISBN 978-1-250-11868-4 (hardcover)
ISBN 978-1-250-11869-1 (e-book)

Our books may be purchased in bulk for promotional, educational,
or business use. Please contact your local bookseller or the Macmillan Corporate
and Premium Sales Department at 1-800-221-7945, extension 5442, or by e-mail
at MacmillanSpecialMarkets@macmillan.com.

First Edition: February 2017

10 9 8 7 6 5 4 3 2 1

Cover and book design by Claire MacMaster, barefoot art graphic design

CAN YOU
SNORE
LIKE A DINOSAUR?

MONICA SWEENEY

with Certified Pediatric Sleep Consultant **LAUREN YELVINGTON**

Illustrated by **LAURA WATKINS**

CASTLE POINT BOOKS
NEW YORK

The Help-Your-Child-to-Sleep Method

BUILD THE FOUNDATION for a lifetime of quality sleep for your little one by establishing healthy sleep habits! Children who are well rested are generally more cooperative and happy. Well-rested children also have a lower risk of obesity, learning challenges, and social-emotional difficulties. Finally, there are practical tools to help your child do just that. You can improve your child's well-being by introducing these sleep habits, all while sharing special moments and a bedtime story.

- **Identify Fatigue:** Be proactive in preventing your child from becoming overtired. Be alert to the first signs of sleepiness: yawning, staring off, glassy eyes, low energy. If your child becomes emotional, cries excessively or "crashes," they have already passed their optimal naptime or bedtime.

- **Set the Stage:** Create a sleep environment that sets the stage for healthy sleep. Freeing their sleep environment from stimulating lights and electronics will allow kids' brains and bodies to unwind. Draw the shades and, if necessary, use

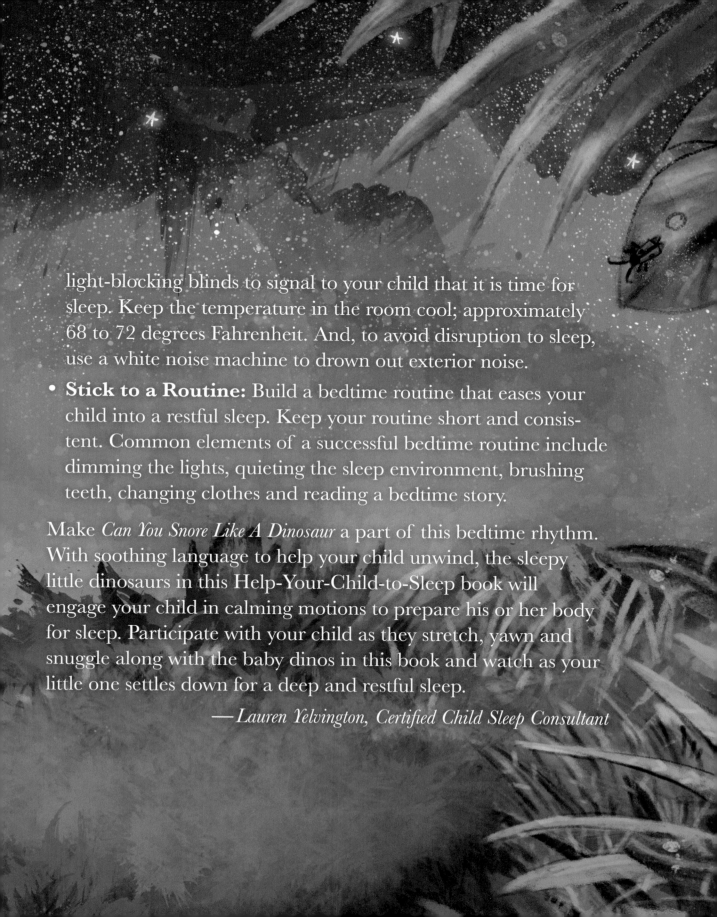

light-blocking blinds to signal to your child that it is time for sleep. Keep the temperature in the room cool; approximately 68 to 72 degrees Fahrenheit. And, to avoid disruption to sleep, use a white noise machine to drown out exterior noise.

- **Stick to a Routine:** Build a bedtime routine that eases your child into a restful sleep. Keep your routine short and consistent. Common elements of a successful bedtime routine include dimming the lights, quieting the sleep environment, brushing teeth, changing clothes and reading a bedtime story.

Make *Can You Snore Like A Dinosaur* a part of this bedtime rhythm. With soothing language to help your child unwind, the sleepy little dinosaurs in this Help-Your-Child-to-Sleep book will engage your child in calming motions to prepare his or her body for sleep. Participate with your child as they stretch, yawn and snuggle along with the baby dinos in this book and watch as your little one settles down for a deep and restful sleep.

—*Lauren Yelvington, Certified Child Sleep Consultant*

Near and far,
far and wide,
all the little dinosaurs
are getting sleepy.

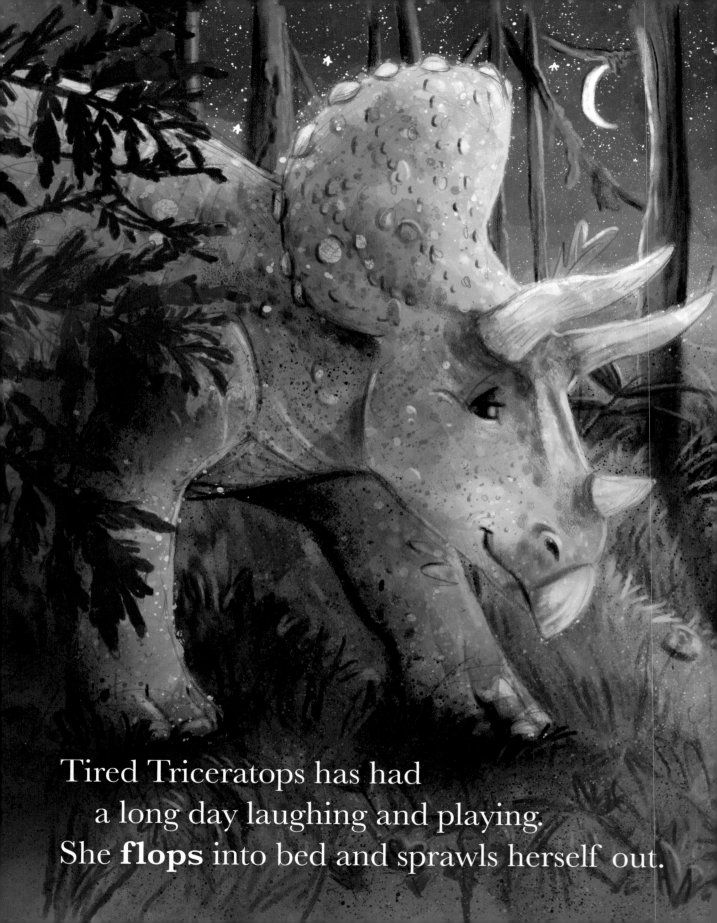

Tired Triceratops has had
a long day laughing and playing.
She **flops** into bed and sprawls herself out.

Can you *flop* like a Triceratops?

Sleepy Steggy is all tuckered out.
She plunks on down and **sighs** a big sigh.

Can you *sigh* like a Stegosaurus?

Happy Apatosaurus munches on trees
and green leaves along the river.
When the sun lowers down,
he curls on up and **nuzzles** into bed.

Can you *nuzzle*
like an Apatosaurus?

Antsy Ankylosaurus
  is having trouble getting comfy.
He spots a soft tuft of grass,
  and burrows on in as **cozy** as can be.

Can you be *cozy* like an Ankylosaurus?

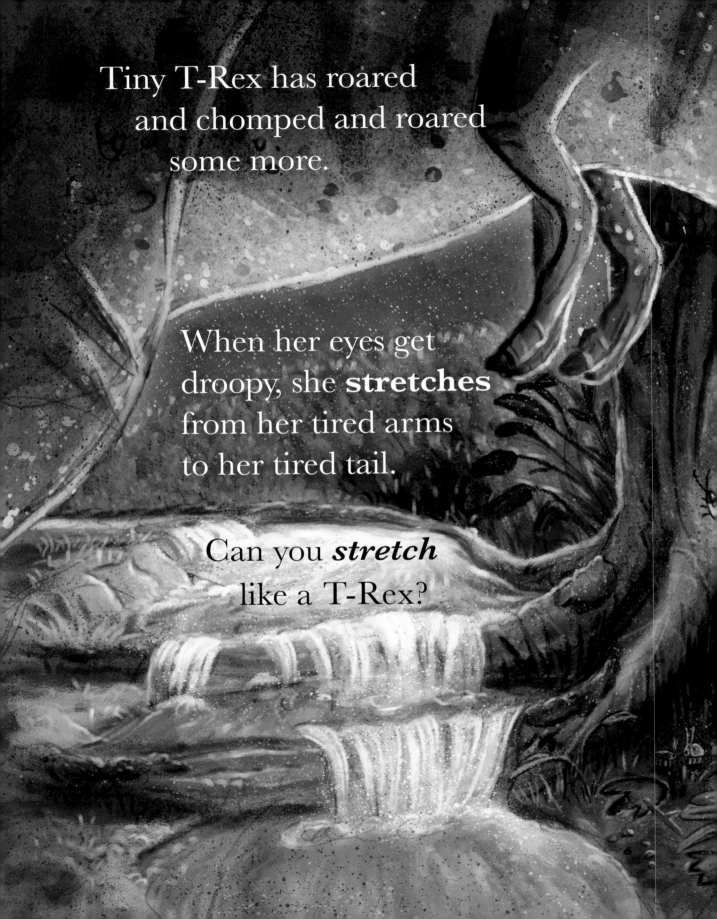

Tiny T-Rex has roared
and chomped and roared
some more.

When her eyes get
droopy, she **stretches**
from her tired arms
to her tired tail.

Can you *stretch*
like a T-Rex?

Baby Velociraptor swishes his tail,
swish swish swish,
from sunup to sunset.
He settles down and **snuggles**
next to mama.

Can you *snuggle* like a Velociraptor?

Itty-bitty Iguanodon
gazes up at the stars.
She watches them twinkle
and **hums** a soft song.

Can you *hum* like an Iguanodon?

Little Liopleurodon
glides through the water
as relaxed as can be.

When she scoots onto shore,
she rests her fins until
they are nice and **calm**.

Can you feel *calm*
like a Liopleurodon?

Dozy Allosaurus shuffles
on the ground and
finds a soothing spot.

He **breathe**s in deeply,
and lets it all out slowly.

Can you *breathe*
like an Allosaurus?

Teeny Pteranodon flaps her wings,
flip-flap, all day long.

When her wings are weary,
she wraps herself up
and **yawns** a sleepy yawn.

Can you *yawn*
like a Pteranodon?

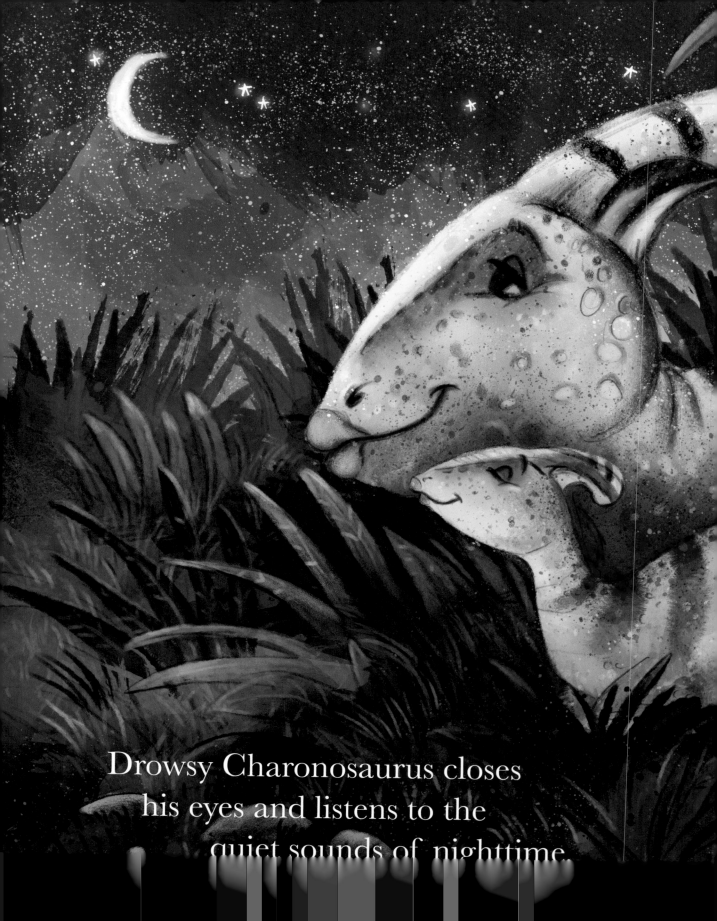

Drowsy Charonosaurus closes
his eyes and listens to the
quiet sounds of nighttime.

He **cuddles** next to daddy,
    drifting slowly off to sleep.

Can you *cuddle* like a Charonosaurus?

Snoozy Supersaurus is
on the edge of slumber,
ready to **dream** her dino dreams.

Can you be *dreamy*
like a Supersaurus?

As the sun goes down,
all the little dinosaurs
have been tucked into bed.
As they fall fast asleep,
they **snore** little dinosaur snores.

Can you *snore*
like a dinosaur?